TODD,

The Flying Penguin

Written and illustrated by Suzanne Moxon

ISBN 978-1-7772307-0-8

WWW.SMOXART.COM

Canada

Down where it's cold
Lived a penguin named Todd.

He was different all right.
He was really quite odd.

The others would watch him
And then wonder why,
This silly young bird
Would stare at the sky.

"It's not fair!" Todd would cry,
"I'm a bird who can't fly!"

"We can swim rather well,"
Replied one of the group.
"Watch me go fast,
And do loop-de-loops."

"Swimming is fun,
I agree with you there,
But it would be great
To fly in the air.

And these aren't wings!"
Said a skeptical Todd,
"They're just fancy flippers.
I feel like a fraud!

A crate washed ashore
Full of wonderful stuff.
Let's make a glider.
I think there's enough."

CAMPING
SUPPLIES

"Just look at this guy
With his head in the clouds!
He's crazy. He's nutty."
They all laughed out loud.

"Why don't we go
And do fun penguin things,
While Todd takes his trash
And tries to make wings."

Already distracted,
Todd picked up a pole.

To sketch a design
Was his primary goal.

"Don't you get lonely?"
He heard a voice say,
"When all of your friends
Just walk away?"

"Sometimes," said Todd,
"Would you like to stay?"

"Maybe I will."
She said with a smile.
"You are pretty strange,
But I like your style.

I'd love to help build
Your flying machine.
That's so exciting!
We'd make a great team."

Todd said "Be careful,
They'll think you are odd,
And by the way,
My name is Todd."

"I know," she replied,
"All of us do.
I like to be different
The same way as you.

And just so you know,
My name rhymes with crazy.
So I do understand.
Just call me Daisy.

And what everyone thinks,
I really don't care.
Let them make fun.
They wouldn't dare!"

Todd told her the plan,
And they worked through the night,
In hopes that by morning,
They could take flight.

Daisy's flippers were flying
As she folded up flaps.
Todd tied them to crossbars
And there was time for a nap.

As the sun started rising
In a rose-coloured sky,
The glider stood waiting —
Ready to fly.

They had to get higher,
So uphill they went,
Pushing the glider,
Until they were spent.

The wind started blowing.
They could feel it race by.
Conditions were perfect.
Would it stay in the sky?

When they looked down,
What did they see?
A big group of penguins
Taking dips in the sea.

All of a sudden,
A shadow appeared —
A giant dark shape,
That filled Todd with fear.

Daisy began waving,
And Todd gave a shout,
"Look in the water!
Everyone OUT!"

But no one could hear him.
They pointed and laughed,
And kept right on swimming,
Making fun of his craft.

Todd grabbed the glider.
There was no time to waste.
He needed to warn them.
He had to make haste.

"Good luck." Daisy said,
And gave some advice,
"Fly over the water.
Don't crash on the ice!"

Todd tied himself in
And though he was scared,
Took a deep breath
And launched in the air.

He hung on with flippers,
And opened some flaps.
Then began steering
By pulling on straps.

GET OUT!

Todd circled around,
And then gave a shout,
"There's a shark in the water!
You have to get out!"

They all paid attention,
But so did the shark.
It leapt from the ocean
In a magnificent arc.

Then Todd decided,
Despite Daisy's advice,
"The big fish can't get me
If I aim for the ice!"

Todd hit the ground
With a terrible sound,
And all of the penguins
Gathered around.

Daisy came running
And said, "Let me through!
I hope you're all right!
You really flew!"

Todd then got up.
And said, "I'm OK."
Then they all cheered,
"YAY! Todd saved the Day!"

"Oh no!" Daisy said,
Looking quite sad.
"Your glider is broken!
Aren't you mad?"

"No." Todd replied, "I need a new plan.
I learned how to glide,
But it hurts when I land."

Then he got busy and nobody laughed.
They even helped Todd build a big raft.

THE END

CPSIA information can be obtained
at www.ICGtesting.com
Printed in the USA
LVHW072346070820
662600LV00021B/394